GW00866447

Best Wishes

Mike Gould

ISBN:9781091159891

ADVENTURES

IN FAIRY WOOD

Written and illustrated

By Mike Gould

The author and illustrator of:

Magic in Fairy Wood

Trouble in fairy Wood

The Amazing Fairy Wood

CONTENTS

CHAPTER 1

Christmas is coming

It was the week before Christmas. Ben and Sue were very excited because their father, who was a farmer, had just finished putting up the Christmas tree in the farm house lounge. The box of Christmas tree decorations was open. Ben and Sue tried to find the fairy for the top of the tree in the box, when their father told the children that he now had to join his friends for the Hunt.

The children stopped what they were doing and looked out of the lounge window, just in time to see their father mount his large grey horse in the farm yard. They could see their mother also watching, from the front door of the house. There were a lot of other people on horses of all sizes. Some of the people were wearing coats that were bright red others had black coats, and some with tweed coats. They were all moving gently around the yard, and talking to each other. Running excitedly around the ground were many dogs with their tails wagging very fast.

A large man in a bright red coat and a big hat, took a small trumpet from his coat pocket and played some very high notes that sounded very much like - 'woo-wee, woo-wee, woo-wee'. As the man played the tune, the horses set off out of the yard, with the dogs running ahead of the horses. One dog at the back of the pack, stopped, looked at Ben and Sue who were still watching through the window, appeared to smile at the children, and then joined the others. When all of the horses and dogs had left the yard, the children returned to the task of decorating the Christmas tree.

Across a field from the farm was a large, and quite thick woodland. The children often spent many happy hours in the wood looking for animal tracks, watching birds, and generally enjoying the area. The children were convinced that on occasions they had seen fairies flying around, especially in summer, so they called the wood 'Fairy Wood'.

In a hedge bank in the wood Mr. Arthur Mole and his Wife Mrs. Mole were entertaining a few of their woodland friends. The jolly group included Mr. Wood the mouse, Walter Vole and Mr. Red the squirrel.

The group were all sat around a nice roaring fire in Mr. and Mrs Moles home. The fire had a big black kettle boiling away over it, from were Mrs. Mole had made some of her famous elder flower tea. She had also baked some oak flower biscuits that were being enjoyed by all.

It was just as Mr. Red the squirrel was about to drink his tea. The whole room shook. Pots and pans fell off the shelves. Walter Vole fell off his chair, a picture jumped off the wall, and a noise like thunder filled the air. The noise and shaking went on for quite a while. Mrs. Mole ran to her husband who held her very tightly in his arms. Mr. Red the squirrel's tea cup was shaking so much that he spilt the tea all over his fur.

At last the noise stopped. The room became still again. The only noise was the kettle boiling over the fire, and Walter Vole's teeth chattering together as he tried to stop himself from shaking.

All the friends in the room looked at each other, each with their mouth wide open in astonishment.

Mr. Wood the mouse stopped shaking and asked, "What on earth was that"? At that same moment, everybody stood very still, for just outside of the door, could be heard a very loud sniffing and snorting noise.

The mole's door is in the side of a hedge bank in Fairy Wood, and is hidden from outside by grasses, weeds and leaves, so it is usually very safe and secret.

Eventually the sniffing and snorting sound from outside the door stopped. Everyone took a deep breath and started to relax. Mrs. Mole picked up the pot and pans, while Mr. Mole hung the picture back on the wall. Mr. Red the squirrel tried to dry his fur with the end of his tail, Walter Vole and Mr. Wood the mouse picked up the chairs that had been knocked over in the confusion.

With everything returned to where it should be, Mr. Arthur Mole stood with his back to the fire, put his hands behind his back and said, "We have had this happen before, but not as bad as it was this time".

"What was that"? Mr. Wood the Mouse asked, still staring at the door with his eyes wide open, for he was very frightened.

"We really do not know what it is. We have had the problem before, and so have some of our other friends that live underground". Mr. Mole replied, trying to be as calm as he could.

Mrs. Mole offered her biscuits to each of the friends, who one by one shook their heads to the offer, as they were all still shaking from the incident.

Mr. Red the squirrel opened his mouth as if to speak, but did not because there was a very loud and fast banging on the door.

Mr. Mole left his place by the fire and moved quietly to the door. He opened the door just a little bit to peer outside. As soon as the door was unlatched, it was thrown wide open to reveal a fox who was totally out of breath. The fox tried to say something, but as he was breathing so heavily he could not say anything.

Mr. Mole shouted to the others, "It's Sky the Fox, and he is exhausted".

Mrs. Mole shouted to her husband, "Let him in, let him in for goodness sake let him in".

Mr. Mole stood aside from the door, and beckoned the fox to come into the house. The fox burst into the room, and ran to the bottom of a staircase in the opposite corner of the room from the door, where he hid behind a wall, breathing so heavily his lips were shaking.

Mr. Mole closed the door, but not before having a good look outside, just to make sure that nobody was watching.

The fox started breathing more slowly. He moved away from hiding behind the wall and stood in front of the fire, looking around at who was in the room with him. The fox was bigger than the other animals so his head nearly touched the ceiling.

Mrs. Mole was first to speak. "What on earth is the matter"? She asked the fox looking very concerned.

"I was chased, I was chased", replied the fox still trying to get his breath back.

"I left my lair to try to find food for my family. I left my Wife at home to look after our three children. I was just not being as careful as usual, because I was wondering what my family would like to eat. I had my head down, sniffing the ground when I found myself looking right into the eyes of a big dog. His tail was wagging very fast. I turned and ran. I ran as fast as I could. In moments I was being chased by huge horses and barking dogs. I just ran and ran. I could see ahead of me a very thick bush of brambles, so I headed straight for it. I dived right into the brambles, and went as deep into the bush as I could. The dogs stopped chasing me. They were running around the bush sniffing and snorting, trying to find me. I stayed as still as I could. At last they went away, so I followed a hedge bank, running as fast as I could. I heard the horses running towards the hedge bank, so I stopped, and stayed very still. The horses were running towards me very fast, and then they all jumped right over the hedge bank, and ran on. The dogs followed them all except one who stopped and sniffed at the hedge bank. When the dog ran on I knew he was sniffing at your door. I know you are all frightened of us foxes, but I knew we had all been friends before, so I had to ask for help".

"Well what a story. You must have been very frightened"? Mrs Mole said to the Fox.

CHAPTER 2

Gone to help

Suc and Ben had been looking out of their bedroom window for a long time, watching the progress of the hunt. They saw the horses and riders going from field to field, jumping over fences and hedges with the hound dogs running beside the horses, following a scent.

The children heard the shrill of the huntsman's horn indicating that a fox had been seen. In a distant field they watched as the dogs set off, followed by the galloping horses. From the bedroom window the children had a good view for quite a long distance. The chase went on and on, from one field to another until the dogs entered the wood near the farm. The horses followed. All was quiet for a while, but then the horses were seen jumping over hedge banks back into the field. The dogs followed. The horses ran on into another field, and into another until they disappeared into the distance.

"Did you see that fox run into Fairy Wood"? Sue said grabbing Bens arm, and pulling him away from the window.

"Let's go and see if we can find the fox", Sue continued pulling Ben out of the bedroom door and down the stairs.

"All right", Ben replied as he was dragged out of the front door by Sue.

As the children crossed the field from the farm towards the wood, they again heard the huntsman's horn in the far distance. They reached the gate at the edge of the wood, and were astonished as a hound dog sped past them with its tail in the air, heading for the sound of the horn.

Ben and Sue entered the wood as they had done many times before. It was a favourite place for the children as they had had many an adventure in the wood. They thought they had seen some magic in the wood before.

The children followed a path deeper into the wood. It was quite cold and muddy along the path. They could see the hoof marks in the mud from the horses, and the many paw prints from the dogs. Ben stopped. He pointed to the ground, and pointed to a different paw print in the mud. Ben had noticed the print was smaller and more pointed than the others. Although it was deep in the mud, it was not so clear, indicating a lot more hair between the toes than a dogs paw.

The children looked around, and saw many more prints the same, but spaced apart, showing that the animal was running very fast. They followed the paw prints until they came upon a large number of them beside a hedge bank. The prints then disappeared.

There was nothing indicating where the animal had gone. The hedge bank was too high for a fox to jump over. So where did he go?

Sue found an old tree stump to sit on, and Ben just looked around trying to find the answer. "Move over and let me sit down as well". Ben insisted as he wriggled to sit on the tree stump next to Sue.

Inside the Mole's house Mrs. Mole was just about to ask if anyone would like some of her famous barley tea, when Mr. Mole put his paw to his lips and said "Sh". Everybody stopped talking, and became very still, and very quiet. As they listened, human voices could be heard outside of the door.

Arthur Mole crept to the door and listened with his ear against it, then, very quietly opened the door, just a little bit. He peered through the gap in the door, and saw the two children sitting on the tree stump. He closed the door again very quietly except for a small 'click'.

"What did you see"? Asked Mr. Red the squirrel, with all of the others staring at Mr. Mole looking for an answer.

"There are two humans on the old tree stump outside". He indicated with his hand pointing to the door. "After everything that has happened today, we really do not want humans causing more trouble", he continued.

"Why don't you use that 'Blue Powder' you bought from the 'Passing Pixy', he did say it was 'very powerful stuff', it might just help", Mrs. Mole said as she reached for the jar of powder from the shelf above the fire place.

Walter Vole passed the jar from Mrs. Mole to Mr. Mole, saying, "Give it a try Arthur, it might just get rid of them".

"No, I don't think so, this powder is far too powerful for us to play with", replied Mr. Mole passing the jar back to Walter Vole.

"Very well then, let's see if this works", Walter Vole said as he quietly opened the door balancing the jar in a paw. He crept outside, and in a flash tossed a small amount of powder onto each of the children. As Walter Vole turned to run back into the open door, he tripped and fell headlong into the mud behind the tree stump.

Ben or Sue did not see the Water Vole carry out his mischievous deed, but they both heard a funny noise behind them. Ben was just about to stand up to investigate the noise, when he saw Sue shrink very quickly right in front of his eyes. Immediately afterwards Ben found himself shrinking as well. In moments both of the children were standing on the top of the tree stump holding on very tightly to each other.

"What has happened", shouted Sue.

Ben replied in a very shaky voice, "I don't Know".

The children peered over the edge of the tree stump still holding onto each other, and there below, in the mud, was a Water Vole with his arms and legs spread out, lying in the mud.

The children looked in amazement at the sight of the Vole. The animal scrambled to his feet, tried to brush some mud from his tummy, looked up at the small children watching him from the top of the tree stump, and fell backwards into the mud, in astonishment at what he had seen.

The Vole scrambled to his feet and ran at high speed into an open door in the hedge bank.

"I think we have shrunk", Ben announced as he realised that they were now standing on the edge of the tree stump, with the ground a long way below them.

Sue whispered "Shrunk? How can we shrink"? She released her tight grip on Ben, and peered over the edge of the stump. "How are we going to get down from here"? She continued, "It's far too high to jump".

Walter Vole burst through the open door into the Moles house, ran to the bottom of the stairs and stood with his back against a wall, where Sky the Fox had hidden earlier, and took several very deep breaths.

Walter Vole asked in a whisper, from behind the wall, "Did anybody see what happened"?

"Yes we did", replied Arthur Mole, still looking through the gap in the open door. "Those humans are the same size as us and they are stranded on the top of the tree stump".

"Well, well, well", said Mr. Red the Squirrel, leaning over the top of Mr. Mole's shoulder, as he looked through the gap in the open door.

Mrs. Mole said in very concerned way, "You cannot leave them on the top of the old stump, they will never get down from there on their own". She pushed past Arthur Mole and Mr. Red the Squirrel, opened the door wide, and went outside to the bottom of the tree stump. "It's all right my dear's", Mrs. Mole shouted to the children, "We will soon have you down from there, - somehow".

The children gasped in amazement, for on the ground below them was a Mole wearing a yellow apron and a cream floppy hat and talking to them, but also, they understood what the Mole had said.

Sue whispered into Ben's ear. "Did you hear that Mole talking to us? Do you think it would understand us if we spoke to it"?

"I don't know, but let's try, because somehow we have to get down from this tree stump, and it's a long way down", Ben replied.

Ben leaned over the edge of the stump and shouted, "Hello, Hello down there, can you hear me, can you hear me. We are stranded up here and can't get down, can you help us"?

Mrs Mole shouted back at Ben, "Don't worry my dear, I will get some help". With that she ran back through the open door in the hedge bank.

Once inside the Mole's house Mrs. Mole asked if anyone had any idea how to get the humans off of the tree stump.

Mr. Red the Squirrel stepped forward and said in a very bold voice, "I can climb trees very well, leave it to me I will get them down, but I will need several bed sheets.

Mrs. Mole disappeared into another room and returned a few moments later with a pile of bed sheets in her arms. Mr. Red the Squirrel took the sheets from Mrs. Mole, and asked the others to help him tie them together from corner to corner. When this had been done, he tied one end to his tail, went out of the door and started to climb the tree stump. In a moment he was on top of the stump standing beside the children, who were looking very frightened at the sight of a red Squirrel as big as they were.

Mr. Red the Squirrel just smiled at the children, untied the bed sheet from his tail, and re-tied the sheet to a convenient wooden splinter. He checked to make sure the sheet was secure by pulling very hard on it.

"Come on follow me", he commanded the children as he slipped over the edge of the stump, holding onto the sheet like a rope.

Sue was first. She crept over the edge holding very tight to the bed sheet, and started to climb down. As soon as Sue was on her way down, Ben followed down the sheet, going arm over arm as he went.

 As soon as they were all on the ground, the Squirrel dashed up the tree stump again, unhooked the sheets and threw them to the floor. In a moment he was standing beside the children again, with a big smiley grin on his face. He gathered up the bed sheets and asked the children to follow him through the door in the hedge bank.

Once through the door the sight that met the children was amazing. They were in a room with a large fire place, with a kettle boiling merrily, away hanging from a hook over the fire. There was a staircase to the left of the fireplace going upwards, and a number of closed doors in the walls of the room. Stood near the fireplace was a black Mole wearing spectacles, a very muddy Water Vole, a brown Mouse, a large Fox, the lady Mole they had seen earlier and the Squirrel who had just rescued them. All of the animals were looking at the children in amazement.

The Mole with the spectacles said, "Hello, I am Mr. Arthur Mole and you are in my Kitchen". Pointing to the lady Mole, and then to the others he continued, "This is my Wife Mrs. Mole, this is Walter Vole, Mr. Wood the Mouse, Sky the Fox, and I see you have already met Mr. Red the Squirrel".

"All very well with these introductions, but what am I going to do with these dirty bed sheets? Mrs Mole announced with her paws on her hips.

Ben thought that everything and everybody seemed very familiar, but could not say exactly what it was, he did think that he had been here before. In a moment he put the thought out of his mind, for he knew that it was not possible. Perhaps it was in a dream.

Sue pulled on Bens arm, and told him that she was a bit frightened.

CHAPTER 3

The Old Crow

Ben spoke first, "What has happened to us? My sister is frightened because we can understand what you are saying, and we seem to have shrunk from our proper size, and we don't know where we are, and we don't know what is happening, all we know about most of you animals is that you squeak when you make noises, and here you are talking to us".

Mr. Wood the mouse replied in a very stern voice, "SQUEAK, SQUEAK, we don't squeak, we communicate in a proper way, we don't SQUEAK".

"I am very sorry", Ben replied, I didn't mean to offend you.

Mr. Mole tried to settle things down by saying, "We are all a bit on edge at the moment, because Sky the Fox has just been chased by lots of wild dogs, and we have had an earth quake above our house, and a big sniffing noise outside the door. You have shrunk because some magic powder was sprinkled onto you. I can now see that it was indeed 'very powerful stuff'. If you can, could you please help us to keep us safe from those big animals, and we will try to help you get back to your normal size again. Oh dear, what a mess we are all in".

Walter Vole stepped forward and said, I think that we must have a plan to get the humans back as they were before, then they will be able to help us".

"What a brilliant idea", said Sky the Fox, "All I want is to be left alone and not chased by those horrible animals, All I want is a quiet life to spend with my Wife and cubs".

"There you are then", Mrs. Mole said, "Why don't we all sit down and have some of my barley tea and some oak flower biscuits".

The group of animals and children sat on chairs around the fire, except for Sky the Fox who stood beside the fireplace, leaning with his elbow on the mantle shelf.

They all talked for quite a long time, trying to think of a way of getting the children back to their normal size.

Mr. Mole eventually said, "In the back of my mind I know what we have to do, I am sure we have done something like this before, but no matter how hard I try to remember, it just will not come to me. I think we have to find Walt the Wizard, I am sure he can help us. But first we have to find the Wood Elders. It is only the Wood Elders who know where to find Walt the Wizard, we should find some of the Wood Elders at the King Oak, but how do we get there"?

Walter Vole all of a sudden stood up straight, and said to Mr. Mole, "Arthur, do you remember that cart you had a few years ago, with the straps. Do you still have it"?

"Yes I do. It is in the store room a bit further down the hedge bank". Mr. Mole replied as he dashed through the door to the outside.

Walter Vole addressed everybody and said, "We have used this before, if it works it will be the best way to get to the King Oak, but it is very dangerous as we have to travel along the floor of the Wood very fast, and there are 'things' out there as well".

Moments later Mr. Mole appeared at the door, "Its outside", he said as he indicated for everyone to come outside and view the cart.

The cart was very interesting, as it was made from twigs and sticks, with slices of cut logs for wheels, and two long arms at one end.

"We copied it from one we saw the humans use", Mr. Mole said standing beside the cart looking very proud of it.

Mr. Red the Squirrel and Mr. Mole set to work with the cart and long lengths of strips of material that looked like rope. They worked with Sky the Fox with great skill. At last it was done. The cart was attached to Sky the Fox by the long arms and the rope like material. It looked just like a horse and cart that the children knew well.

Walter Vole got onto his hands and knees beside the cart, so that the others could use his back as a step to climb into the cart one by one. The cart was just large enough for all to sit on its floor, until Walter Vole jumped on board, when it became quite a tight fit.

Sky the Fox looked behind him at the group of animals and children who were squeezed into the funny looking cart. He gave a smile, and set off along the path.

Ben leaned towards Sue and whispered into her ear, "Have you noticed that it is not winter any more? The trees and bushes have leaves, and there are flowers growing. This really must be a very magical wood. I feel quite warm. It was winter when we came into the wood, do you remember, that it is one week before Christmas"?

Sue looked around her, and sure enough the season had changed, the leaves on the trees above them were giving a welcomed shade from the hot sun, and summer flowers were everywhere. Sky the Fox was now running quite fast along the paths, weaving between bushes and trees. The cart was bouncing along with its passengers being tossed from one side of the cart to the other. Mrs. Mole was holding onto her hat as they sped along.

After quite a while Sky the Fox stopped in a clearing. "We have arrived at King Oak", he announced. In the centre of the clearing was a very large and very old Oak tree. Walter Vole jumped out of the cart and again got onto his hands and knees beside the cart. He indicated for the others to use his back as a step to climb out of the cart.

"You are very kind Walter", Mrs. Mole said as she stepped from the Voles back to the floor.

Mr. Red the Squirrel and Mr. Wood the Mouse were busy undoing the ropes securing the cart to the Fox. The children noticed there were some steps going from the ground to a closed door in the side of the big tree. Mr. Mole climbed the steps and knocked very hard on the door. There was no answer so Mr. Mole knocked again, but harder this time.

Almost as soon as Mr. Mole stopped knocking the door opened wide and a badger appeared wearing a long black butlers coat and a white bow tie.

"Can I help you"? The badger asked in a stern butler's way.

Mr. Mole asked if the Old Owl or any of the other Wood Elders were able to see him, as it was very important.

The badger told Mr. Mole that nobody was in today, not even the Old Crow who was the Old Owl's assistant. "What I do know is that the Old Owl is visiting some Witches today, I think he was going to see Witch Big Feet, and Witch Forgetful. Witch Forgetful should be at fairy Dell, if she remembers to go".

"Thank you very much", said Mr. Mole, as he climbed back down the steps, leaving the badger to close the door. "Looks like we have to go to Middle Wood", he announced to the group. "We should be able to get help there".

Ben was now starting to get very concerned that they were not going to get back to normal quickly, and asked Mr. Mole where Middle Wood was, and how to get there. Who was Witch Big Feet, who is Witch Forgetful, and why is it now Summer; for when they came into the wood it was Winter?

Mr. Mole replied that, "This wood is very magical. The moment you shrank you became part of that magic. When the wood becomes magical it is always summer, and you see different things in different ways. Magic has a way of making things different. To find Middle Wood we now have to go underground. Follow me please". He indicated for the group to follow him along the path.

Partly hidden by a large bush was a flat rock. One edge of the rock was held up by another rock. This arrangement made an entrance under the flat rock. It was a very well used entrance as there was a lot of paw and foot prints leading to under the rock. Sue looked inside the opening. She could see bright lights deep under the rock.

"Come on follow me", insisted Mr. Mole as he walked under the flat rock. Mrs. Mole followed her husband followed by Sue, Ben, Mr. Wood the Mouse, Walter Vole, and with Mr. Red the Squirrel at the rear. Sky the Fox decided to make his own way home through the wood, as he knew that some of the areas the others will be passing through will be far too small for him to go.

Once well under the rock they found themselves in a tunnel with earth walls and ceiling. The tunnel was lit at regular intervals by glow worms stretching along the tunnel floor, near the walls.

It was amazing how much light the glow worms provided, for the tunnel could be seen a long way ahead, as it wriggled its way further and deeper beneath the surface.

The group continued on their way down the tunnel, following Mr. Mole all the way. They passed a group of pixies playing skittles with acorns. The pixies were shrieking with laughter because when thrown, the acorns did not go in the direction intended, as they were not a round shape. The pixies did not notice the group passing because they were so involved in their game. Sue pointed to the pixie group as she passed, as she thought she had not seen pixies before, but she could not be sure about that.

At last they came to a large open space, with high ceilings, and benches for sitting on around the edge of the cavern.

Ben looked all around the cavern. There were four tunnels going in four different directions in the walls of the cavern, including the tunnel they had just come along. Many different animals and creatures were in the cavern. There was a mouse with a haversack on his back, a rat walking backwards and forwards with a news paper under his arm, several mice chatting together and sitting on one of the benches. There were voles, moles, Gnomes, bigger water voles, hedgehogs, pixies and elves. There were also some creatures that Ben had never seen before. All seamed to be waiting for something. On the wall of the cavern was a sign, it said 'Fairy Dell'.

Mr. Mole found an empty bench, so he indicated for everyone to sit on the bench with him.

"What is Fairy Dell"? Ben asked as he sat beside Mr. Red the Squirrel.

"This is Fairy Dell station", Mr Red the Squirrel replied pointing to the sign on the wall. "We have to catch an Ant Coach to get to Middle Wood", he continued.

Sue sat next to Ben and held his arm very tightly, as she watched the other animals and creatures in the cavern. Sue's thoughts were stopped by the sound of what seamed like thunder coming from one of the tunnels, there was also a huge draft of wind coming from the tunnel. Sue held onto

Ben's arm even tighter as she stared into the darkness of the tunnel.

In a moment, eight very large ants arrived from the tunnel, pulling some funny looking open coaches. They did look a bit like coaches and horses, Sue thought. The ants and coaches stopped in the centre of the cavern, covered by a cloud of dust from the dry dusty floor.

Two adult squirrels and two little squirrels climbed out of one of the two coaches, along with what looked like a person surrounded by steam. The person surrounded by steam sat on the bench next to Walter Vole.

CHAPTER 4

The Misty Witch needs help

Walter Vole started coughing very loudly, for the steam from the person sitting next to him got into his throat.

"Sorry about that", the steamy person said as it moved a bit further away from Walter Vole. "I'm going to Witches junction to get my steam sorted out", it continued. "I am the Misty Witch and I should have mist around me, not steam, It's very hot in here you know with all this steam, something has gone wrong so I am going to get it put right. Where are you all going, and who are the humans with you, or are they elves dressed to look like humans"?

Walter Vole told the Witch that the children were elves in disguise going to a fancy dress party, and they were trying to reach Middle Wood. They have a problem and need to meet with the Wood Elders for help.

"Oh you mean Walt the Wizard", the Witch replied. "He is the most respected in this wood you know, and he knows everything there is to know. Very difficult to find though, but I do know he has been trying to help the Wet Witch, as she has a bit of a problem with dampness like me".

Sue noticed the coach and ants had some new passengers, as some of the Gnomes who were waiting in the cavern were now sitting in a coach. Right at the back of the last coach was a mouse wearing a yellow cap with a peak, and a role of tickets on some string around his neck. When the gnomes were sitting safely he blew on a whistle. The ants stood up straight after their rest, and set off at high speed into another tunnel. As the coaches set off, the mouse ticket collector fell head over heals out of the back of the coach. He picked himself up, and was last seen running after the coach, blowing his whistle and waiving his arms in the air.

Ben thought there was something familiar about the ticket collector, but he could not think what it was.

Shortly the dust settled in the cavern, as it did so another loud noise and huge wind came from another tunnel. Moments later more coaches arrived in the cavern, again pulled by eight of the largest ants the children had ever seen. They were nearly as big as a mouse. A coach stopped beside the group, so Mr. Mole followed by Mrs. Mole, Walter Vole, the Children, Mr. Wood the Mouse, Mr. Red the Squirrel and the Misty

Witch all climbed into a coach. They all sat on very spongy seats. When all were settled a whistle was blown at the front of the first coach, but no mouse ticket collector could be seen.

Sue managed to look through the others on the coach, and could see a yellow peaked cap, under the cap was a mouse. The mouse appeared to be very sleepy, and was curled up on a front seat, with his hat pulled over his eyes.

The coach sped into a tunnel. It was travelling so fast that it appeared to be flying. As the coach went around one corner after another, the spongy seats were very welcomed, as the passengers were thrown from one side to the other. The speed of the coach increased, and the wind passing the animals made their fur fly backwards, and their ears and whiskers to be blown flat against their faces. Nobody could talk, as the noise of the wind passing by was so loud. At one point the coaches flew over a deep ravine with just a narrow path across it. The coaches then dived into another tunnel at what seamed to be an even higher speed. All of the passengers were behaving as though this was normal, A rat in the other coach was reading his newspaper, and a small vole was asleep on its mother's lap. The steam from the Misty Witch was like a smoke trail behind the coaches, and around the corners behind them.

At last the coaches slowed down and stopped in the middle of another cavern, very similar to the one they had left.

The mouse ticket collector was now awake and shouted "Witches Junction. Next stop Middle Wood. Thank you". He then curled up on the front seat again, put his head down, his tail around his neck, pulled his hat over his eyes, and started to snore very loudly. His snoring was so loud that the small vole woke up wondering what the noise was.

The Misty Witch jumped out of the coach. A sizzling noise could clearly be heard coming from the Witch, as she hurried towards a tunnel, with a signpost saying 'workshops this way'.

Mr. Mole said "Ours is the next stop. It won't be long now". He smiled and settled back onto his spongy seat.

When all the passengers who wanted to get off, had got off, and new passengers were on their seats, a squirrel at the front, put his paws in his mouth and gave a shrill whistle, because the mouse ticket collector was still snoring loudly.

Immediately the coaches set off again, dashing into a nearby tunnel.

Again the coach seamed to be flying at high speed through the tunnel. Every time the coach went around a corner Sue had to hang onto the side because the seat was so spongy she was wobbling all over the place. The coach entered a new large cavern that was very brightly lit, but it did not stop, in fact it did not even slow down. Again it dashed into another tunnel and continued on its reckless way.

At last Ben thought the coach was slowing down. It entered yet another large cavern, and stopped in the middle, much to the relief of Sue, who was looking quite pale from the wobbling about.

Mr. Mole indicated for them to get out of the coach and headed for a wooden door in the side of the cavern. Beside the door was a sign saying, 'Middle Wood enquiries'.

Mr. Mole opened the door and went in followed by the others. He seamed to know where he was going, so the children were happy to go with the others.

Once through the door there was a staircase going upwards, with a rope attached to the wall as a handrail. The stairs went up for a long way.

At last they were at the top, and they found themselves in a room with many Elves working away at desks. All of the desks were full of piles of papers.

Mr. Mole went straight up to one of the desks with a sign on it saying, 'Wood Elders Reception'.

The group of friends surrounded the desk where an Elf was busy working with his head down.

"Oh, oh, can I help you"? The Elf announced with a jump, as he realised that he had a group all around him.

"We need to see the Wood Elders urgently", Mr. Mole told the Elf who was looking at the strange group of animals and humans around his desk.

"Urgently"? The Elf replied. Well now, if you need urgent then you need the help of a Witch to get you there. He found a book on his desk, and opened it to a well worn page. He looked at the page with his finger following the words. "Ah here it is", he continued. The Elf put both arms in the air and said some words that nobody understood. Immediately standing beside him was a very beautiful woman with bright gingery red hair.

The beautiful woman smiled at the group and said, "Hello, I am Witch ----, Oh dear who am I "? She asked the Elf.

"Forgetful. Witch forgetful", the Elf replied.

"That's right". The woman continued. "I am Witch Forgetful. Oh dear I do forget the most silly things sometimes. So, I understand you need to see the Wood Elders, urgently". She smiled at the group again and clapped her hands three times.

In the time it takes to blink an eye the group of animals and children were sat around a large table in a large room with curtains hung on the walls, and silk sheets on the ceiling. At one end of the table was an Owl sitting on a lovely chair. The Owl was wearing spectacles on his beak. He had a large golden book open in front of him, and he was studying it with interest. Standing on the back of the chair was a large and very black Crow. The crow seamed to be smiling at Ben, but Ben thought crows can't smile, but this one was.

The Owl gently closed the book, sat back in his chair, and looked at the group.

"How can I help you"? The Owl asked as he pushed his spectacled further back onto his beak.

Mr. Mole told the Owl about the hunt horses jumping over the hedge banks, about the dogs sniffing outside of their door, and about Sky the Fox until he was so exhausted he could hardly breath. He then told the Owl about the blue magic powder that had shrunk the children, and that they need to know how to return the children to their normal size.

The Owl scratched his head with the end of his wing, thinking. At the same time, the crow was walking backwards and forwards across the back of the chair, copying the Owl by scratching his head with the end of his wing. The crow was so intent at copying the Owl, that when he got to the end of the chair, he kept walking and fell right off the end. Because he was using his wing to scratch his head, he could not use it to fly, so there was a large 'thud' as the crow hit the floor.

There was a flutter of wings from under the table, and the crow had returned to the back of the chair, looking very embarrassed.

The Owl looked at the crow very sternly as if he was not very happy, then said to the group, "You have several problems, so I think we need to deal with them one at a time. I need to see about these horses that are making you frightened. To do this I must see them from the air, as well as the hedge bank where you live. I will need you to show me were you live and where the horses might be".

Mr Wood the mouse asked the Owl how he could be shown all this when nobody except the Owl could fly.

The Owl replied. "I have already thought of that. Do you remember the days when people thought babies were delivered by storks? Well, a little while ago I bought a used carry hammock from a passing stork, before it flew off to a warmer country, and I have it stored in a cupboard. Because it is not very big it will only take a light load. I suggest you Mr. Mouse as you are the lightest, to show mc the hedge row, and the two children to show me where the horses might be. Please fetch me the carry hammock Mr. Crow". He pointed to a door with his wing.

"I do not like this idea at all", Walter Vole announced, "Is it not easier to go under water".

Mr. Red the Squirrel almost shouted. "Don't be silly, you are the only one who can swim, anyway, where is there any water"? Walter Vole folded his arms and placed his chin on his chest, as he did feel very silly having made the suggestion.

The crow produced the carry hammock from the cupboard and placed it on the table.

The Owl said to the others, "We won't be very long as I fly very fast, so you could all have a snooze in the chairs until we return. But you are not allowed to look in my golden book".

The Owl hopped onto the floor and walked towards a door, with the carry hammock in its beak. He indicated for the children and Mr. Wood the Mouse to follow him through the door.

As the children went through the door they were amazed, because they both thought they were way underground, instead the door was in the side of a large tree trunk, and they were in the warm sunshine somewhere in the wood. The Owl placed the carry hammock on the floor and asked all three to sit in the middle of the hammock. The Owl flapped his wings and hovered over the hammock. He picked up the hammock with his long sharp claws, gave a few flaps of his wings, and they were in the air.

CHAPTER 5

A Bad Spell

The Owl flew with expert skill through the wood with the children and Mr. Wood the Mouse peering over the side of the hammock, and hanging on very tightly. The hammock was very safe in the claws of the Owl as they darted through the wood at high speed, missing trees and bushes as they went.

The Owl asked Mr. Wood the Mouse to shout when he recognised the area where the hedge bank was. Ahead there was a clearing in the wood, so the Owl flew upwards through the clearing until they were high above the trees in the wood. The Owl flew on and on at high speed.

Ben looked all around, and in the distance could see the farmhouse. He shook Sue's arm and said, "Look we are nearly home; let's get him to drop us off".

Sue shouted in return, "That's no good, we are still too small. We can't go home yet".

Mr. Wood the Mouse pulled one of the Owls feathers on his leg, and pointed ahead and below.

The Owl nodded his head and dived towards the ground. Mr Wood the Mouse again pointed ahead, so the Owl started to slow down. Eventually they were flying in circles above the hedge bank.

Back in the Owl's room, Mr. Red the Squirrel noticed that the crow was fast asleep, with his head tucked under his wing, while still standing on the back of the chair. He gave Walter Vole a nudge with his elbow, and pointed to the crow. Mr. and Mrs Mole were both also fast asleep in their chairs.

Mr. Red the Squirrel hopped onto the table and crept on his toes towards the golden book that was right in front of the sleeping crow. As he crept along the table, there was a loud snore from Mr. Mole. Mr. Red the squirrel stopped moving. The crow appeared to wake up, but put his head under his other wing, and started to snore quietly as well.

The Squirrel moved forward again, but more slowly this time. Walter Vole was watching from his chair and waiving his arm at the Squirrel as if asking him to return to his seat. The Squirrel was now right in front of the book. It was very beautiful, with lots of gold squiggles on the cover. The naughty squirrel opened the book to the first page. He could not read any of the words in the book as none of them made any sense.

The Owls spectacles were beside the book, so Mr. Red the Squirrel put them on hoping he could see the words more clearly. All of a sudden he could see the words, so he turned to a different page. Although the words were clearer he still could not make any sense of them. So he began to read the words aloud.

"Grun koop mool shoop fluggl", he whispered to himself. But it still did not make any sense. So he continued, "Molop upla suroog". The Squirrel stopped reading, for the table, chairs and all of the animals started to shake. The table shook so much the Squirrel fell onto his back. By now everybody was awake and hanging onto the table very tightly.

The table and chairs stopped shaking, all the lights went out, and it was as dark as dark could be.

Mrs. Mole shouted, for she was very cross, "Now look what you have Done Mr. Red".

The Squirrel responded, "I can't look, its all gone dark".

Indeed it was so dark that not a singe thing could be seen, by anyone. Walter Vole started to walk about with his paws stretched out in front of him. He could not feel anything. Then; all of a sudden; the lights came back on again, and they all stood very still, with their mouths wide open in surprise at the sight they saw. Standing right in front of them was a very large and very ugly looking Witch. She had an enormous nose, big eyes, lots of large crusty lumps all over her face, one large tooth on her bottom jaw poking out of her lips and upwards towards her nose, and whiskers on her chin. The Witch was much bigger than any of the others, and she glared down at them all. Mrs. Mole noticed that the

Witch had very large shoes that seamed to have a lump at the toes.

The Witch said very sternly, "Who called me? I was having a wonderful sleep until I was called. What is so important that you had to wake me up"?

The Witch pulled the owl's chair away from the table and sat down. Even when sitting down she was still very large. She noticed the open golden book on the table and the words that Mr. Red the Squirrel had spoken.

"I see", the Witch said pointing to the words on the page. "Someone has been messing about with things that they should not be messing about with".

The Witch raised her arm and pointed her finger at each of the friends. The finger stopped when it was pointing at Mr. Red the Squirrel. "It was you", the Witch exclaimed making her knobbly finger shake towards the Squirrel.

Mr. Red the Squirrel put his paws over his face and said in a squeaky voice, "I didn't mean too. I was only looking. I didn't mean too, it was an accident".

The Witch wriggled in the chair, she started to reach out with her arm towards the Squirrel. The arm got longer and longer, until it was right over the Squirrels head, who was standing at the other end of the table. The hand became huge, and scooped up the Squirrel in one singe move. The Witch swept the Squirrel back to place him on the table, right in front of her.

"You must learn not to mess about with things that you should not mess about with", the Witch said with her face very close to the Squirrels. "I think that I must now teach you a very important lesson. As you obviously like magic, I will give you sticky fingers. That will teach you".

"OH NO", shouted the Squirrel, "We are on a very important quest, and the Old Owl is helping us. Please don't punish me. It will cause us all lots of problems, not just us but many others in the wood. Oh please don't punish me it really was an accident.

The Witch winked her left eye at the squirrel and left in a cloud of pink smoke.

"Thank goodness for that", said Mr. Red the squirrel sitting on one of the chairs around the table. "I think that I got away with that very well", he continued scratching an itch he had on this right ear. It was at this stage that the squirrel squealed with fright. His finger was stuck to this right ear. He pulled as much as he could but it was stuck fast.

"Don't touch anything else" shouted Mrs. Mole as she ran to help the frightened animal.

Moments later a door opened and the Old owl flew into the room carrying his passengers. He gently placed all his passengers onto the floor, and flew to sit again on his chair.

"What has been going on here while I was away" the Owl asked in a very stern voice, glaring at the frightened squirrel.

Mr. Wood the mouse took a deep breath, thankful that they were all back safely. Then realising that something was wrong, decided to hide behind a convenient curtain.

Arthur Mole spent quite a long time telling the owl in detail how the squirrel came to have sticky fingers.

"I think we need to see the Witch again, don't you? If I knew which spell the squirrel read from my golden book then I could recall the right Witch. Can anybody describe the Witch, was there anything about her that was odd?".

Again Arthur Mole explained to the Old Owl that the Witch was very large. With large feet and hands.

"Ah ha", exclaimed the Owl. "That must be the Big Witch. Now I know the right spell to get the Witch back again".

The Old Owl opened his golden book, turned to the correct page and began to read, "Grun koop mool shoop flugg molop upla suroog".

As the Owl finished reading the spell the lights went out, the room shook in the darkness, and a very loud 'THUD' was heard. When the lights came on again the reason for the noise was clear, for the Big Witch was sitting in the middle of the table holding her right foot.

"Who called me when I was trying to cut my toe nails? Very glad you did interrupt me because I just cannot reach my toes".

The Witch let go of her foot and looked around the room at the surprised animals and children.

"Oh it's you again". She exclaimed crossing her legs and arms while still sitting in the table. She really was very big and took up most of the table top. "So who read from the golden spell book this time?" I think someone else needs sticky fingers for messing about with things they should not have been messing about with".

"It was me who summoned you". The Old Owl said as he sat vey upright on his chair, trying to look bigger than he really was.

"I know that you were trying to teach the squirrel a lesson for being naughty, and I understand your reasons. But this time these animals really are on an important mission. So could you please unstick the squirrel so that they can all try to help the Fairy Wood?"

The Witch wobbled for a moment on the table as she uncrossed her legs. She looked at the squirrel and winked her left eye at him. Moments later the pink smoke appeared again and the Witch was gone. Mr. Red the squirrel who had been pulling very hard to release his paw from his ear, found he was at last free. He ran to join the others looking very shocked and vowed never to mess with things that do not belong to him ever again.

CHAPTER 6

Elfingham

When all was settled again after the Witch incident, the Old Owl said that he has seen the area where the problem had been with the horses and dogs had occurred and that he was sure that Walt the Wizard was the right Wood Elder to help the group.

The crow, who had been sitting on the back of the Owls chair, and watching the proceedings with great interest, thought that he should not play with the golden book either as he might also have sticky wings.

The Old Owl thought very hard for a moment, pushed his glasses firmly back onto his beak and hopped from the chair into the floor. He went to a large drawer filling cabinet in the corner of the room. He opened a drawer and to everyone's astonishment the head of an Elf peered over the top of the drawer, with a beaming smile on his face.

"Phew, nice to get some fresh air", the Elf said taking a deep breath of air into his lungs. "I suppose you need some information", he continued while filing his finger nails with a large nail file. "Every time you open the filing cabinet you stop me filing my nails, oh well, what is it this time"? The smile on the Elf's face seemed to be fixed as his expression never changed.

The Owl asked the Elf where Walt the Wizard was now and how can the group get to where the Wizard was?

The Elf scratched his forehead with a long finger nail, leaving a red mark where he had scratched himself, then disappeared down into the cupboard. Moments later the Elf appeared again holding a piece of paper.

The Elf passed the paper to the Owl and again disappeared deep into the drawer.

"Um ", said the Owl reading the paper with his glasses perched on the end of his beak. Today it seems Walt the Wizard has gone to visit an area of the wood called Elfingham with a group of young Elves. He does this every year so that he can teach the young Elves a few magic tricks, just to keep them out of trouble. Elves are naturally naughty creatures and need things to keep them occupied. Elfingham is where lots of

Elves live and play. If you manage to get there please be careful of the Elves as they can be very mischievous. You can get to Elfingham by taking the 'Loop' road".

"Thank you very much". Said Mr. Mole. "So where is the 'Loop' road please".

"When you leave this tree by the front door the Badger butler will show you the way". The Old Owl said as he hopped back onto his chair, put his head under a wing and went fast asleep, snoring with a slight whistling noise.

Sue and Ben had been watching everything that had been going on with amazement. They had seen things that they had never seen before, but it all seemed to make sense.

Mr. Mole led the way back through the door they had previously entered the room by, went down a steep flight of stairs and right up to the front door, followed by all of the others. Walter Vole decided that he just wanted to keep out of the way when in the Owl's room, just in case something nasty happened to him, so he was last in the group to reach the front door.

The Badger butler was there to meet them all. He opened the front door and pointed to a small footpath that led deeper into the wood. They all went through the door and down the steps to the path below. Ben turned around to look at the tree. How did all of that part of the adventure occur inside the tree trunk, he thought, as it was just not big enough. Must be magic he concluded.

It was still high summer in the wood, the trees and bushes were all shades of green and bluebells lined the sides of the footpath they were told to take.

The path was just wide enough for the friends to travel side by side. As they walked along the path Ben noticed there were ripe apples on some trees and yet there were also bluebells on the ground. He knew that bluebells come in the springtime and apples are ready in the autumn. He thought it very odd that there were two seasons together. He knew the wood was a magic wood so accepted the strange things he saw.

As they walked they talked about the events in the Old Owls room and the strange Witch they had seen. Mr. Red the Squirrel often touched his ear, just to make sure it would not stick to his hand.

They had walked for some time when they came across a fairy sitting on a rock beside the path. She was making a very long daisy chain with very big daisies. As the group came nearer she stopped her work and smiled a big smile.

"Hello", said Mr. Mole to the fairy. "Are we on the right path to Elfingham".

"Don't know" answered the Fairy in a miserable sort of way.

"Are you all right"? continued Mr. Mole.

"I'm fine thank you. I am Lolly the lazy fairy so I am always like this. I am never able to enjoy things because I am always too lazy to be bothered", she replied.

"Ah ha" said Mrs. Mole as she pushed her way to the front of the group. "You need stinging nettle tea, that will revive you to a happy energetic fairy. Now all I need is some nettles and some water. Everyone have a look around and see if you can find some".

Sue found the nettles first. The leaves were much bigger than those she had seen before, but then she realised that she was small. The hairs on the back of the leaves that sting could clearly be seen. She shouted that she had found the nettles, so Mrs. Mole expertly picked the leaf without being stung, and crushed it between two stones.

Walter Vole is an expert in finding water which he did with ease, flowing from a rock that was covered in damp moss.

Mrs. Mole collected some water in her hat and added the crushed nettle leaves. As she squeezed her hat a liquid dripped out.

"Come and drink this", Mrs. Mole asked the fairy. So the fairy drank some of the liquid dripping from the hat. She then sat down again on her rock looking very glum. Mrs. Mole sat beside the fairy on the rock, and talked to her for a long time. The others sat on the path and rested.

After a while Mrs. Mole Stood up to join the others, but as she did so the fairy grabbed her by the arm and said that the tea had started to work.

She was now feeling much better and her laziness was going.

Mrs. Mole was very pleased that the nettle tea had been successful, however her hat was now in a bit of a mess. Mrs. Mole returned to the rock where the water was flowing as if it were a spring. She washed her hat in the flowing water, squeezed the excess water from the hat and allowed the light breeze to dry the hat.

Meanwhile the others had been chatting to Fairy Lolly and discovered that they were on the right road to Elfingham and that they should all be very much aware, because when there are a lot of Elves together they become very naughty.

Mrs. Mole returned to the group and was very pleased to see that the Fairy had recovered very well.

"Better get a move on", Walter Vole said as he started to walk along the path.

They all were going to say goodbye to the Fairy, but she had disappeared.

The sky above the trees was very blue, and sun rays flashed on the path through the leaves and branches. Sue and Ben began to feel very tired but the others hopped and skipped their way along the path. The path took a very sharp right turn, and there in front of them was a high bank with no other way out apart from the path they had come along. In the side of the high bank was a wooden door with large hinges. Guarding the door was an elf. He was standing in front of the door with his arms folded and looking very official.

Walter Vole recognised the elf, he moved forward and said to the elf "Hello Henry, haven't seen you since you let us borrow your magic upside down table. How are you and what are you doing here"?

"Oh hello Walter". The elf replied pushing his chest forward and his shoulders back, trying to look as important as he could. "I'm here on guard keeping unwelcomed people away from Elfingham. This is my turn so I am doing my best".

"I see", Walter Vole replied, "Well we are here on official business", he continued, "We need to see Walt the Wizard as soon as possible to sort out a big problem in the wood.

"You might say that, but how do I know that is true". The elf said pushing his chest even further forward.

Walter Vole took one step closer towards the elf and reminded him about the time the elf let the group borrow the magic table, when that was an important time.

"I do remember very well, so this time it must be very important as well", the elf replied uncrossing his arms and letting his chest return to normal. "I will let you in but you must be very careful as all sorts of things can happen in there".

The elf went to a ticket machine that was on a table beside the door, he turned the handle seven times and seven tickets came out of the machine all joined together. He gave the tickets to Walter Vole and opened the door using a very big old fashioned key. Walter Vole was first to enter the door followed closely by the others. When all of them had gone through the door it closed very loudly behind them.

All of the friends stood together and stared in amazement at the sight in front of them.

They had passed through the door to the other side of the bank into an open grassed area with the blue sky above. But, they have never seen so many elves in their lives. Lots of them were sat on the grass playing games like chess, tiddly winks, lotto, and dominos, other were playing with a bat and ball, a tennis racket and a football.

Sue was just about to say that none of them seemed to be naughty when she felt things going on behind her. Sue has long blond hair, 'and in moments her hair was platted into two plat's and tied together at the ends, and Ben had his shoe laces tie together so that he could not walk, Mr. Red the squirrel found he had bells tied to his bushy tail and Mr. Moles glasses had disappeared and were now on Walter Voles nose. Yet none of the elves seemed to have moved from the games they were quietly playing.

A tiny elf jumped in front of Mr. Wood the mouse as if to play a trick on him, but the mouse hopped out of the way to be behind the elf. The elf turned this way and that way but could not see the mouse because the mouse was always behind the elf. The mouse was just as quick at moving as the elf. Eventually the elf stopped twisting and turning, scratched his head with a bony finger and ran away.

Ben untied his shoe laces and then Sue's hair, Mr. Red the squirrel took the bells off his tail and Mr. Moles glasses were returned to him.

A very fat elf stopped paying chess with another elf and wandered slowly to stand in front of the group. "Do you want to play with us today or do you want us to play with you"? He asked.

Mr. Mole adjusted his glasses and told the elf they were trying to find Walt the Wizard as he could help them with a big problem that was affecting the wood. The elf smiled at Mr. Mole, turned around and walked away back to play chess again without answering.

"Well that was a lot of help" sighed Sue looking at all of the unhelpful and uninterested elves. "They are a naughty lot of elves", she continued.

Mr. Wood the mouse noticed a group of Gnomes sitting on chairs at the far end of the field. "Let's see if we can get some help from them"? he indicated to the Gnomes.

So the group made their way through the elves towards the Gnomes. They had not gone very far when Mr. Red the Squirrel fell flat on his face. Two elves ran away collecting some string that they had used to trip the squirrel.

Mr. Red the squirrel picked himself up from his fall and ran the rest of the way to the Gnomes followed by the others.

Mrs. Mole arrived right behind the squirrel and asked a rather fat Gnome if he knew where Walt the Wizard was.

The Gnome appeared to wake up from a doze, looked at the group with sleepy eyes, and went back to sleep again with an enormous snore without answering Mr Moles question.

A group of four fairies flew over a nearby hedge and landed right in front of the group. One fairy said to them that they had obviously been having trouble ever since they entered Elfingham and did they want some help.

CHAPTER 7

A Different Place

Mr, Mole again explained to the fairies about the problem they have with the horses and dogs, and that they are trying to reach Walt the Wizard for help.

"You need to go to the Wizards monthly meeting at Wiz lodge, That is where he is now, but to get there you must all walk in a squircle". She continued.

"What on earth is a squircle"? asked Walter Vole.

"Fairies normally either walk or dance in circles to cast spells, but as you are not fairies then you must walk in a squircle to make the spell work. Hold hands in a circle then squeeze in and out to make it a square, then walk to the left keeping the shape of the square. That is a squircle".

The group followed the instructions given by the fairy. A cloud of sparkly yellow dust filled the air around the group. When the dust settled they found they were inside a large room with no windows, but the room was very light.

A very small man dressed in a green coat and wearing a black top hat was standing on a pile of books talking to a group of very odd-looking Witches.

As the group of animals and children arrived, he turned around on the pile of books that wobbled as he turned. He lost his balance and fell to the ground with a 'thud', landing on his back.

"Hello", said the little man as he stood up again onto his feet, "Who are you"?

"We are trying to find Walt the Wizard, because we have a big problem, and we hope that he can help us", Mr Mole said looking down at the very small man.

"Well you have found Walt the Wizard for I am he" Said the little man trying to compose himself after his fall.

Sue touched Bens arm and whispered that she did not like being in this place.

Walt the Wizard heard Sue's comment, so he clapped his hands very loudly. All the lights went out. It was very dark. Then very slowly the light came back until it was very bright and everyone could see that it was the sun shining above them

They were all standing on very warm sand. Behind them were steep tall cliffs, and in front of them was the loud rolling waves of the sea.

"Is this better"? the Wizard asked Sue. She nodded her head in agreement.

Mr. Wood the mouse pointed to the sea and said to Walter Vole, "You like water, there is plenty of water there".

"Oh no", replied Walter Vole, "That is salt water, no good for me I'm afraid, I can only swim in fresh water, river or pond, I don't mind".

Mrs. Mole lifted the bottom of her skirt and paddled her toes in the cold sea water. As everyone was very small the waves coming onto the beach appeared to be very big, so she just stood right on the edge as the water came to meet her feet, and watched as the water disappeared back into the sea.

Mr. Mole watched his wife from a dry distance, with his hands on his hips and shouting to her as a new wave started to come ashore.

Mr Red the squirrel was jumping up and down and shouting that he did not know where he was as he had not seen this before and that this sandy stuff was getting into his fur.

Mr. Wood the mouse and Walter Vole were sat on a large rock watching the scene with interest.

Ben and Sue held hands and just watched the rolling sea.

After a while Mr. Mole remembered why they came to see Walt the Wizard. The Wizard was looking at the rolling sea with his hands clasped behind his back. "It's a long time since I have seen the sea", he announced to Mr. Mole who was now standing beside Walt the Wizard.

Mr. Mole agreed with the Wizard and continued, "Can I please tell you why we came all this way to tell you about our problem"?

Mr. Mole then told the Wizard the whole story about the horses frightening the small animals, the hound dogs that sniffed at the entrance to their homes, how the children became involved and the adventures they had trying to find Walt the Wizard.

"You all have had an adventure", the Wizard exclaimed in surprised at the effort all of them have made. "Must be very important to you all to come all this way". I think I can help you with the problem of the horses and dogs, but you must all return to your house as soon as possible. When you get there, you must give the children three drops of dew from a snowdrop, this will return them to their own world. I will now cast a spell that will be like a magnetic fence. Gather your friends together and hold hands in a circle. I will then ask you to close your eyes".

Mr. Mole thanked the Wizard and collected all of the friends. While still on the beach they all held hands in a circle, and when told by the Wizard they closed their eyes. With eyes still closed they all noticed the sound of the sea was gone. Mr Wood the mouse was first to open his eyes and shouted in amazement. All the others opened their eyes to find they were all outside of Mr. and Mrs. Moles front door.

Mr. Mole found a snowdrop with plenty of dew in the petals. Before he gave the dew to the children, they all noticed that the wood had returned to winter time, and it was very cold.

"We would all like to thank you Ben and Sue for your help, as we now know how to make you into our world and to return you to your world, you are welcome at any time". Said Mr. Mole. He then gave each of the children three drops of dew from the petals. Immediately both children found themselves growing very fast until they were the correct size. They were both sitting on a tree stump beside a hedge bank. There was no sign of any animals or the Moles front door. The air was chilly. Ben asked Sue if they had had a dream or did an adventure really happen. Sue told Ben that she was very sleepy but was now cold and wanted to go home in the warm.

The children returned home to the farmhouse. The children's Mother made some hot coco, and both children sat on the sofa next to a roaring fire. Just before evening the children's father returned with a few friends after their day out hunting on horses. Their father and his friends sat around the big dining table talking about the day out.

One of the friends said that every time the horses or dogs came near to the old wood, that the animals would not get close to the wood no matter how hard the riders tried. It was almost as if a strong magical fence was around the wood. The other friends agreed and all said they will not go near the wood next time as it would frighten the horses too much.

Ben and Sue just looked at each other and smiled. Was this the work of Walt the Wizard or was it all a dream?

THE END

Printed in Great
Britain
by Amazon

32438253R00050